MIJ KELLY AND ROSS COLLINS

WHERE GIANTS HIDE

Hodder
Children's
Books

A division of Hachette Children's Books

I went hunting for giants.

I searched far and wide.

They're bigger than houses.

So **where** do they hide?

Where
is
the
fairy
who'll
grant
me
a
wish?

And **what happened** to mermaids?

Did they **turn** into fish?

When I try kissing frogs,

they **don't** turn into princes.

If I try riding **broomsticks,** they **won't** budge two inches.

So don't say there's a **troll** lurking under the bridge.

Don't tell me that goblins are raiding my fridge.

Or that magic is knocking **tip-tap** at my door...

because I don't **believe** it exists any more.

If it did, we'd have pixies
to keep the house clean,

terrible
dragons
to make us all
scream,

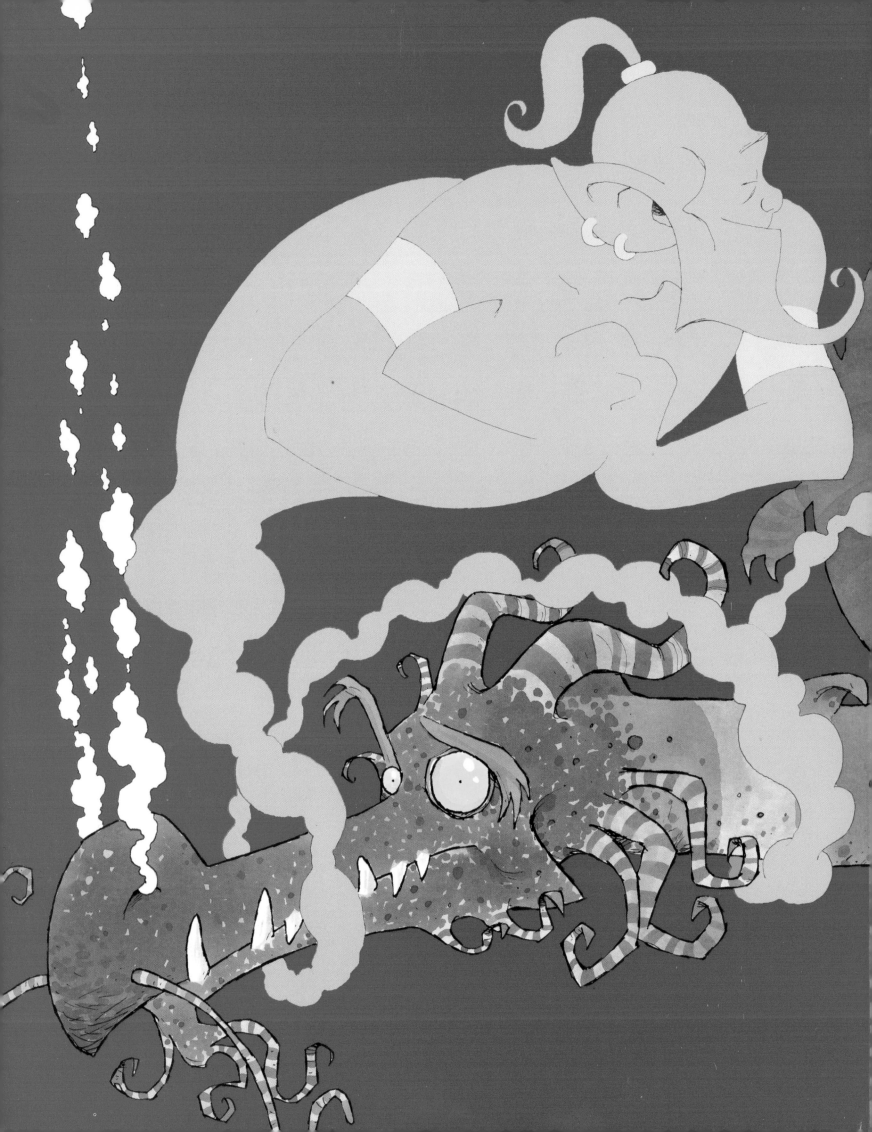

and strange, see-through genies like great puffs of steam.

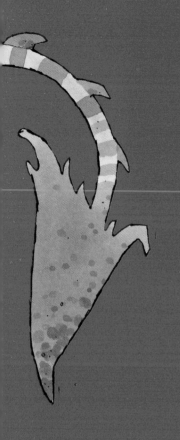

But these things aren't **real.**

The world's dull and grey
and if there ever was **magic,**
it's
all
leaked
away...

And
that
makes
me
sad.

How **I wish** that, right now,
the world would stand up
and take a **big bow**,

and do something
.
amazing...

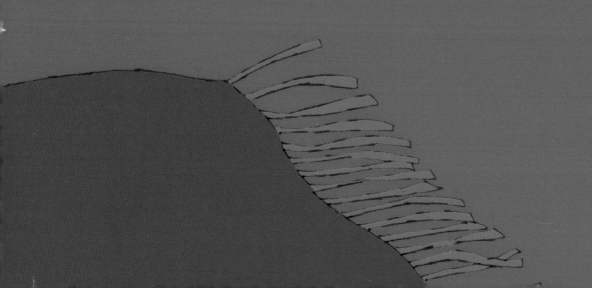

...to make me go 'WOW!'

Something amazing, especially for me.
And that's when I wonder, hey,
what would it be?

And that's when I see
I can dream it alive,
and that's when I know...

Oh! That's where giants hide!

To Ralph - M.K.

For Nick, Sam, Ruby and Finlay - R.C.

by Mij Kelly
and Ross Collins

First published in 2009 by Hodder Children's Books

Text copyright © Mij Kelly 2009
Illustration copyright © Ross Collins 2009

Hodder Children's Books
338 Euston Road
London NW1 3BH

Hodder Children's Books Australia
Level 17/207 Kent Street
Sydney, NSW 2000

The right of Mij Kelly to be identified
as the author and Ross Collins as the illustrator
of this Work has been asserted by them in accordance
with the Copyright, Designs and Patents Act 1988.

A catalogue record of this book is available
from the British Library.

ISBN: 978 0 340 95999 2
10 9 8 7 6 5 4 3 2 1

Printed in China

Hodder Children's Books
is a division of Hachette
Children's Books.
An Hachette UK Company

www.hachette.co.uk

www.rosscollins.net